A Tree in Sprocket's Pocket

Stories about God's Green Earth

Paulette Nehemias

Illustrated by Jim Harris

CONCORDIA®

PUBLISHING HOUSE

Stories about God's Green Earth

A Tree in Sprocket's Pocket
Wiggler's Worms

✶

A Tree in Sprocket's Pocket
is printed on recycled paper.

Scripture taken from the HOLY BIBLE, NEW INTERNATIONAL VERSION®. Copyright © 1973, 1978, 1984 by International Bible Society. Used by permission of Zondervan Publishing House. All Rights Reserved.

The "NIV" and "New International Version" trademarks are registered in the United States Patent and Trademark Office by International Bible Society. Use of either trademark requires the permission of International Bible Society.

Copyright © 1993 Concordia Publishing House
3558 S. Jefferson Avenue, St. Louis, MO 63118-3968
Manufactured in the United States of America

Library of Congress Cataloging-in-Publication Data

Nehemias, Paulette, 1958–
      A tree in Sprocket's pocket: stories about God's green earth Paulette Nehemias; illustrated by Jim Harris.
      (God's green earth; bk. 1)
      Summary: In this collection of short stories with accompanying activities, children confront environmental problems and learn to care for God's earth.
      ISBN 0–570–04730–7
      1. Children's stories, American. [1. Environmental protection—Fiction. 2. Christian life—Fiction. 3. Short stories.] I. Harris, Jim, 1955– ill. II. Title. III. Series.
[PZ7.N423Tr 1993]
[Fic]—dc20   92-26033
                                                                              CIP

1 2 3 4 5 6 7 8 9 10   02 01 00 99 98 97 96 95 94 93

Contents

A Tree in Sprocket's Pocket

As his Uncle Walt's truck rounded the corner, David peered through the windshield to see if his grandfather's tractor was parked in the shed. Unless Grandpa was riding one of the horses, the parked tractor and the car next to the garage were sure signs that Grandpa was in the house. Everyone said David and his grandfather were just alike. Grandpa thoroughly enjoyed time spent with his grandson, and David felt as if he and his grandfather always wanted to do the same things. Depending on the time of year, a weekend with Grandpa might include going to a baseball game, planting trees on Grandpa's tree plantation, target shooting with Grandpa's .22, or maybe fishing on the stream that flowed into the nearby Sandusky River. And of course, enjoying Grandma's wonderful cooking was something they did any time of year.

This past spring Grandpa had celebrated his seventieth birthday. Although he still rode Yankee Paul bareback, he complained of aches and pains that slowed him down. About five years earlier, he had told David's dad that he felt like a gear that was missing a cog or two. That was about the time that David was old enough to start helping Grandpa with different projects at the tree farm. Grandpa dubbed him "Sprocket," a nickname that stuck. Sprocket seemed to be the missing cog to help Grandpa get his projects done just a little quicker, and David's company made any job more enjoyable.

Grandpa was never lacking for projects on his farm, even though he rented out all the crop fields to a young farmer. His passion was the 40 acres of woods beyond the pastures and fields. Grandpa managed the woods as a tree farm. To Grandpa, that didn't mean just raising fields of trees. It meant that he took care of the woods to enhance the wildlife and produce strong, healthy trees. His goal was to maintain a lush, natural area to be enjoyed by people, animals, and trees.

Sprocket was Grandpa's tree-farmer-in-training. He already knew how to plant a seedling, untangle the choking honeysuckle vines from young saplings, and identify the chrysalis of the destructive bagworm.

On this day, as Uncle Walt's pickup neared the Ohio farm, Sprocket was especially excited to see Grandpa. This weekend trip had been arranged suddenly, before Sprocket got home from school. Mom said she was visiting a friend for a few days, and Dad needed some time alone. Sprocket would go to Grandpa and Grandma's, and his two sisters were going to an aunt's house.

Sprocket knew something was up. His mom and dad had been spending an unusual amount of time talking behind closed doors, and things seemed very tense around his house.

Although Sprocket had lots of questions, he kept them to himself. He wasn't sure he wanted to know what was going on. Mom and Dad hadn't been getting along for a long time. Now Mom was staying with a friend. If things stayed like this, then his parents would be separated. It was really too soon to think like that, but he couldn't help it. He wanted things to be all better. He didn't want to think about what might happen next. Sprocket was hoping a weekend away from his family's townhouse would take his mind off Mom and Dad's problems. If things were bad at home, there was no place else he would rather be than at Grandpa's house.

Grandpa heard the truck as it turned into his driveway. He hurried to meet his grandson in the driveway. They hugged briefly.

"Did you hear what we did at school this week?" asked Sprocket. Before Grandpa could answer, the enthusiastic boy continued, "We planted trees along the Johnny Appleseed Highway. My whole class was there. A forester taught us how to plant the trees; but of course,

I already knew how." He stopped just long enough to catch his breath. "They were big trees, Grandpa. They must have been 10 or 12 feet tall! The roots were in a big ball of dirt, wrapped with burlap. They were too heavy for us to carry without lots of help. We planted 75 trees this week! We worked all morning, and after lunch some kids just stayed on the bus and goofed off, but not me. I helped all day." That was no surprise to Grandpa. He was all too familiar with how hard his grandson could work.

As they walked to the house, Grandpa realized that Sprocket hadn't said anything about the situation at his own home. That would come later, Grandpa was sure.

Sprocket recognized the warm, spicy smell as soon as they were on the porch. Grandma's cookies were baking in the oven and, as on every visit, Sprocket passed the embroidered stitchery hanging in the entrance:

Who plants a seed beneath the sod
And waits to see, believes in God.

No doubt about it. He was at Grandpa and Grandma's house. It felt good.

Uncle Walt headed back to town before the cookies were done, so just Grandpa and Sprocket were at the table when Grandma brought over a plate of still-warm cookies. While she moved about the kitchen, Sprocket finished telling his grandfather every detail of the exciting tree-planting adventure. It was a lot harder planting the big crab apple trees next to the highway than it was planting trees at Grandpa's.

These same two cookie-eaters had planted almost 400 trees just last year on Grandpa's farm, but those trees were just little sticks with a few hairy roots on them. Grandpa pointed out the area where he wanted the trees planted, and one push with your foot on the shovel made a deep slit in the rich soil. Forcing the shovel handle away widened the slit enough to slide in the roots of the tiny tree. Pull out the shovel and tamp down the soil to close the slit, and that was it. A young tree had a new start. Move over 8 to 10 feet, repeat the process, and another tree was planted.

Sprocket talked a mile a minute while gobbling up another cookie. School was fine, his huge baseball-card collection was still growing, he had taken his first babysitting job, and his newest interest was hockey. Street hockey to be specific. Grandma shuddered.

No mention was made of the mysterious happenings at Sprocket's house, with his mom gone and his dad wanting to be alone. Sprocket and Grandpa thanked Grandma for the cookies and headed out to get their coats. It was time to feed the horses. As Sprocket passed the stitchery about believing in God, he started thinking about the message. In silence they headed to the barn.

The young boy and older man measured out grain, dropped hay from the loft, and checked the water level in the tank. They were listening to the contented munching of the satisfied horses when Sprocket finally asked, "It doesn't matter if you believe in God, does it?" He didn't wait for an answer. "I mean, the Bible tells us not to worry and all that, but it doesn't matter. Bad stuff still happens."

His grandfather waited to see if he had more to add. Sprocket continued. "We plant trees in the spring, and so does your neighbor. We say we believe in God, and your neighbor says that God doesn't exist. It seems to me that if there's a drought, his trees are going to die, but ours will die too. So what difference does it make? It doesn't make any difference."

Sprocket turned and headed toward the ball field he and his cousin had built on the farm. He didn't look back to see if Grandpa was following, so Grandpa thought it best to let the boy be by himself for a while.

Grandpa knew that Sprocket was wondering about his parents. What was going on? Why was it happening? What would happen next? Even if Sprocket did ask, his grandfather wouldn't have any answers for him. At this point nobody had any answers. As Grandpa climbed up the back porch steps he prayed, "Lord, You be with my son and his family. Let them know You are there for them. Fill them with Your Spirit, so they can get through this together."

Grandma was just hanging up the phone as her husband came into the kitchen. Without going into detail, her son had explained that he and his wife had been at odds over something for a long, long time. Katie finally felt she had to get away. Tom was exhausted from the ordeal and just wanted to rest. The good news was that they were both talking with people who could help them. Their goal was to work through this crisis. Before he'd said good-bye, Tom reminded his mom to tell Sprocket how much he and Katie loved him.

Grandpa sighed as Grandma told him about the phone call. He went to sit in the living room until Sprocket came in, or dinner was ready, whichever came first. He picked up the Bible on the coffee table and shook his head at how tattered the cover looked. It was his own mother who used to say that a Bible that is falling apart is owned by a person whose life is *not* falling apart. That made him think of his grandson out on the ball field. Did he think his life was falling apart? Probably.

Grandpa heard the screen door slam. "Grandma!" called Sprocket. When Grandma answered, Sprocket quit shouting and explained his dilemma. He had remembered that his teacher at school was getting married this weekend. Miss Russell had been his most favorite teacher ever. He wanted to get her just a little something that was extra special. He didn't have much money to spend, but now he wouldn't be able to go shopping at all.

Grandpa, who had been listening from the other room, chuckled to himself. Of course the kid had no money. He spent it all on baseball cards and equipment for his ball field. He also noticed that Sprocket didn't ask his grandparents to take him shopping. Although they would have taken him without hesitation, shopping was not a favorite activity for either of his grandparents.

The main topic for dinner that night was the perfect gift for Sprocket's teacher and her new husband. Nothing was said about Sprocket's mom or dad until dessert. Grandma brought out a blueberry cobbler, and as

Grandpa reached for the cream, she reminded him not to use too much. Grandpa made a puckery face, shook his head from side to side, and in a high voice mimicked his wife, "Remember your high blood pressure." Everyone laughed. It was the first time Sprocket had laughed since he arrived.

"How do you stay married?" he asked suddenly. "You two have been married forever, and mom and dad have been married for a long time, and my teacher is just starting out. I want to get her a special gift that will last forever, because I hope she stays married forever. But not everyone stays married." Then he was quiet.

Grandpa was sure Sprocket was thinking about his own parents. Grandpa left the room and came back carrying the old, worn Bible. He carefully set the book on the table, looked around for his glasses, which he always found on his neatly arranged desk, and then sat down to read.

"Let's see, Jeremiah 17," he said as he flipped the pages. All sat silently until Grandpa said, "Yes. This is it." And he began to read. "'Blessed is the man who trusts in the Lord, whose confidence is in Him. He will be like a tree planted by water that sends out its roots by the stream. It does not fear when heat comes; its leaves are always green. It has no worries in a year of drought and never fails to bear fruit.' "

Grandpa took off his glasses and rubbed his eyes. He was silent for a long moment and then started to explain. "Earlier you asked me what difference it makes to believe in God, and now you want to know about commitment. To me this verse explains both. God doesn't say, 'Blessed is the man who trusts in the Lord, nothing bad will ever happen to him.' No, He says here that the man who trusts God is like a tree with deep roots that reach water. Heat will come and droughts will happen, but God will see him through."

"If the tree represents a person, then what does the stream represent?" asked Grandma.

"Good question, my dear. What do you think, David?"

Sprocket was silent. He bit his lip, and then

thought out loud. "If a man is like a tree, and a tree's roots have to be near the stream to get water, then the water must be something or someone who can help the man get through the tough times. Like maybe his family or friends."

Grandpa raised his eyebrows. "Good thinking, but the beginning of the verse doesn't tell us to trust in our friends and family. The first part says, 'Blessed is the man who trusts in the . . .' "

"Lord!" blurted Sprocket. "We trust in the Lord." He smiled because he got the answer right, but then he sighed. "But, Grandpa, I don't always feel like I trust in the Lord. Sometimes when I pray, I'm not sure if I'm really talking to someone or not. It's easier for me to trust you and Grandma, or Mom and Dad during . . . droughts. And right now, I'm not even sure if I can trust Mom and Dad. I don't know what's going on. I know they're not very happy. Everyone tells me they'll work everything out. But I'm not sure, and I feel scared."

Grandpa stood up and went to the cupboard. He rooted around in a drawer until he found a pencil and paper. It was easy to see he was in a hurry to explain something to Sprocket. Even before he sat back down he started drawing. First, he drew two parallel lines diagonally across the paper. "This is the stream," he explained. Then he drew a picture of a small tree. The roots of the tree were not long enough to reach the stream. "This is me, when I was a little boy. My family talked to me about God, but I was like you. When I was about your age, I wasn't so sure God was really there for me. Maybe He was something parents made up so that we would be good. I didn't feel close to Him like I do today. Thankfully, at a time when my roots didn't reach the water, God saw to it that His water reached me." Here Grandpa drew little stick figure people carrying buckets of water from the stream to the little tree.

"God spoke to me in His Word. He spoke to me when I was baptized. He spoke to me through the teaching of my parents and my Sunday school teachers. And I started to grow! God kept me close to Him."

With a flourish, Grandpa lengthened the

roots of the young tree, stretching them out to the stream. He added longer branches and more leaves. "Eventually, God helped my roots reach the stream, and I did feel very blessed indeed. I feel happier than all get-out when I think about God's relationship with me!"

"Sprocket," he added in a quiet, confident voice. "You are a young tree, planted by a river. God's helping your roots to grow. You keep your sights on the river, and your roots will reach it sooner than you think. You'll see that God's been hearing you all along."

Grandma added with a smile, "And don't ever forget, Sprocket, that your family is always here to share God's love with you." Sprocket sat with his chin resting on his fist. He studied Grandpa's drawing. He was still thinking about it later that night when he went to bed.

The next morning, Grandma and Grandpa were already up getting breakfast ready when Sprocket came leaping down the steps. "Grandpa," he almost yelled, "I've got an idea for my teacher's present. Could you give me a young tree? We could dig it up and wrap the roots and dirt in burlap, just like the foresters did with their big crab apple trees we planted along the Johnny Appleseed Highway."

Grandpa smiled, "That tree will grow and grow, just like your teacher's marriage."

So on Sunday night, when his dad came to get him, Sprocket carried home a tiny, 12-inch tree, with its roots not only balled in burlap, but wrapped in a festive piece of fabric and tied with a matching ribbon and bow. That was Grandma's contribution. Tied to the ribbon was a card that Sprocket had worked on for most of the afternoon. It was decorated with a winding stream, two trees, and lots of brightly-colored flowers. On it was written the words from Jeremiah 17:7–8. Sprocket had used his absolute best handwriting and was pleased with his efforts.

Sprocket walked into his classroom Monday morning and pulled the little tree from his pocket. Miss Russell was delighted. Every teacher and parent who saw the gift seemed moved by the words and by the tender, little tree.

As Sprocket watched everyone's delight with the little tree, a new idea clicked. He could order a hundred baby trees from a nursery like Grandpa did year after year. Then Sprocket could plant them in individual pots and wrap the pot with a pretty piece of fabric, a ribbon, and a bow. He could make a card similar to the one he had given his teacher and make 100 copies of it. Then he would tie a card to each tree, and sell them at the church bazaar.

As Sprocket put his plan into action, he wrapped each tree's roots in peat moss and placed each tree in a plastic bag, with the stem of the tree sticking out. He tied each bag with a ribbon and attached a copy of the card he had designed with the words of Jeremiah 17 on one side, and directions for planting on the other.

Selling the little trees turned into a profitable business for Sprocket. He bought his fill of baseball cards and began to purchase equipment for his newest interest—hockey. He attacked his tree business and his hockey practice like a forward attacks the puck. Yet at the back of his mind, there was always an unspoken prayer: let Mom and Dad stay together. They continued to see counselors, but things were still tense at home.

Spring came, and Sprocket began to dream about going to a summer hockey camp just a few hours away in Michigan. It was too expensive for his parents to send him, and he didn't want to cause any more problems in their already strained relationship. Sprocket's gears began turning, and with Grandpa's help, he came up with another tree scheme. It was a stroke of sheer marketing genius.

Sprocket ordered another 100 flowering dogwood trees from the nursery and started planning a costume—an old battered saucepan; a pair of old, leather work boots; some jeans; a Bible; and a fabric bag that his mother sewed to resemble the shoulder bag that Johnny Appleseed might have carried. Just like the Bible-toting, apple-seed-planting, legendary man with a mission crisscrossed the state of Ohio with a saucepan for a hat, Sprocket planned to do the same with dogwood trees in his neighborhood.

The bundle of bare twigs arrived from the nursery on a Friday afternoon in early April. Sprocket filled a bucket with water to keep the roots of the trees moist while they were at his house. He spent the weekend going door to door dressed like Johnny Appleseed. He was quite the sight with his worn, leather shoes; saucepan hat; a Bible clutched in one hand; and his pouch of little trees slung over his shoulder. Just for effect, he stuck the root ends of two trees in plastic bags and carefully slid them into his hip pockets.

Sprocket boldly strode up to each door in the neighborhood and confidently knocked three times. The surprised persons who answered their doors enjoyed what they saw and heard. Sprocket tipped his saucepan hat and bowed ever so slightly, then began,

"My name, it is Sprocket.
I've a tree in my pocket
Selected 'specially for you.

"It will grow and survive,
Green and alive,
A delight for the world to see.

"Five dollars will buy it.
Go ahead, try it,
And add new life to your yard.

"My name it is Sprocket.
I've a tree in my pocket,
A dogwood or two, for you!"

By Sunday evening, Sprocket had sold half of his trees. He spent the next few afternoons carefully planting the trees where his customers ordered. For each little plant, he dug a hole with plenty of room for the roots to spread out. Before he filled the hole with soil, he mixed in a little of his grandfather's special all-natural fertilizer. Sprocket finished the tree-planting ritual just like his grandfather had taught him. He carefully stepped down on both sides of the tree to firm down the soil. It felt good to be working like his grandpa. Later he would return with some mulch to help the soil hold water, and prevent grass and weeds from choking out the fragile tree.

Sprocket established a tree route for himself in his large neighborhood, much like some other kids had newspaper routes. He cared for the trees he had planted, and offered to cut the neighbors' grass. As summer approached, Sprocket had more than enough work to pay his way to hockey camp. He was delighted.

As Sprocket raced up and down the hockey field, the trees in his neighborhood were spreading their roots underground. Lots of changes were taking place in the trees—and in Sprocket's family as well.

When Sprocket returned from hockey camp in August, his parents were still living together and still working with individual counselors. They were going to give it their all, knowing God's love and forgiveness would help them rebuild their home. And through it all, God's Spirit kept Sprocket's faith growing. He was like that tree planted by water. God was close by, and he had nothing to fear.

Even Grandpa was sometimes amazed at the energy his grandson devoted to trees. "Do you think you'll ever get tired of planting trees?" he asked.

Sprocket shook his head. "I imagine I'll always have enough energy to plant a tree," he answered. "But if I ever do need to rest in a bit of shade, I know about a thousand spots that will be just perfect."

MAKE A GIFT OF A TREE

A tree can be an appropriate gift for any occasion. Trees clean the air, improve the soil, and provide food and shelter for wildlife. Buy a potted tree at a nursery. Wrap the pot and add a ribbon and bow.

Use words from Sprocket's favorite Bible verses, Jeremiah 17:7–8, to make a card.

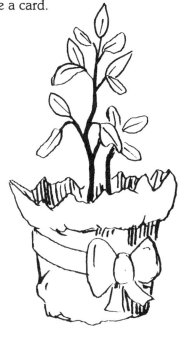

Blessed is the man who trusts in the Lord, whose confidence is in Him. He will be like a tree planted by the water that sends out its roots by the stream. It does not fear when heat comes; its leaves are always green. It has no worries in a year of drought and never fails to bear fruit. (Jeremiah 17:7–8)

Bear Scare

Ryan turned around to see the view behind him. They'd been hiking up the mountain less than an hour, but already the family car looked like a Matchbox toy in the lot below. Beyond the ribbon of highway that entered the area, Ryan could see a patchwork quilt of different shades of green. There were the rough-textured pine forest areas, the delicate-looking cherry orchards still not fully leafed out, and all over were acres of farming fields.

Ryan would have felt content to gaze at the view for hours, but already his brother and sister and father were well ahead of him. Even his mother had passed him up. That was unusual. Usually it was Mrs. St. Pierre who brought up the rear of the family's hiking troupe. She was fascinated with the plant life in these mountains. From the mightiest ponderosa pine to the tiniest alpine blossom, Mrs. St. Pierre was in awe of the splendor and beauty of each unique creation.

The entire family looked forward to these hiking trips. Four-year-old Billy would make discoveries—seeing things that he had never ever seen before in his life! Mr. St. Pierre enjoyed the exercise after spending most of his week hard at work behind a desk. He always seemed to have his eye on the destination, though, and missed much of what his family saw. Marlene and Mrs. St. Pierre were both fascinated with the scenery of the trips. Marlene's favorites were wide panoramic views from earth to sky, from side to side, as far as the eye could see, and her mother's favorites were up close and usually tiny. If the mother and daughter both took cameras on a hike, they would each come home with a completely different set of pictures.

Usually, though, it was Ryan that remembered the camera. He was the observer in the family; he'd be the first to quietly notice a deer in the distance or be able to tell that a bear had passed by recently, because of the fresh scratching marks left behind on a tree. He enjoyed pointing out new discoveries to his younger brother.

Just as the family entered a wooded area, they passed a fire watchtower that overlooked the entire area. Billy said *that* was where he would run if he ever saw a bear. But Ryan said, "That's probably where the bear would run if he saw you first!"

Ryan had just finished reading a book about Denali National Park for a report on Alaska. He had learned that bears had poor eyesight, but a keen sense of smell. If they heard people coming they would most likely head the other way, unless they felt threatened. The book gave a complete explanation of what to do if you should encounter a bear in the woods. It said some people carried bells with them when they hiked in the woods so they could be sure to not accidentally surprise any bears. Ryan was sure that Billy and their dog Greta made enough commotion to frighten away any nearby bears.

By the time the whole family gathered to take their first break, the family had hiked into a sheltered glen. The spectacular view of the valley was temporarily out of sight, and the destination of their hike was around a bend and up yet another long hill. Greta enthusiastically crumpled herself to the ground between the two brothers. She seemed to be smiling as she panted contentedly and loudly. Marlene poured a bowl of water for the dog, and the whole family laughed when Ryan started imitating Greta so he could get a drink too.

"You're being Greta!" declared Billy. "Do someone else."

Ryan thought for a moment and then stood up and strutted in a determined way. He never looked to the right or the left as he pretended to hike around the family. Billy couldn't guess who he was.

"You're Dad," said Marlene, and her father chuckled, a little embarrassed about his hiking style.

Next, Ryan stood still and peered into the distance. He squinted his eyes and shielded his face with his hands. After he took a few steps forward to get a better look at whatever he was seeing in the distance, he pretended to realize that he was about to step off of a cliff. The family laughed as Mr. St. Pierre said, "That's Marlene, without a doubt."

Billy added, "Yeah, she's going to fall down the hill, because she isn't watching where she is going."

Already, Ryan had begun his last impersonation. He was bent over at the waist, studying some imaginary discovery on the ground. Before he could continue, Billy jumped up, "That's Mom! That's Mom! I always think she found something really cool, like a snake or salamander, and it's always some dumb old plant or something."

After a nice rest, the dog was the first to get up. Greta looked back at the family and then trotted ahead to the trail. Mr. and Mrs. St.

Pierre were still reclining in the grass as the kids got up to follow the dog.

Mr. St. Pierre reminded them not to go too far down the trail and said that he and Mom would be along in a minute.

The three walked on around the bend, but could not see any sign of Greta. They called and whistled, but the dog had disappeared. Finally, they heard a bark in the distance. They all went off the trail to the right, where they were sure the barking came from a large grove of pine trees.

Without warning, Greta ran from the grove into the clearing where the children stood. Without stopping, she passed the children and ran straight to the trail, back around the bend from where they had just come. The three turned their heads back from watching Greta's mysterious behavior and froze as a large black bear ambled into view less than a stone's throw away from them. Ryan realized the bear hadn't seen them yet and grabbed Billy as he turned to frantically run back to Mom and Dad.

"Don't make a sound," he urgently whispered. "Start backing up, slowly."

For the longest few seconds ever, the three tried to back away from the nearsighted bear without being seen, and they may have been successful except for the breeze that carried their scent to the bear's sensitive nose. They took a step or two more, until Billy saw that the bear had stopped and was lifting his snout up to smell the air. The bear turned and saw the three frightened children.

"Do exactly as I say," commanded Ryan. "Don't run. And don't make a sound until I tell you. Even if I talk, you both keep silent."

That'll be easy, thought Marlene. I'm scared speechless.

Billy had no choice but to trust his older brother. He was too young to realize what great danger they were in, but he knew from Ryan's tone of voice that he'd better obey.

Ryan tried to speak quietly and confidently, "It's okay, bear . . . We were just leaving . . . See? We're backing up, see? It's okay. It's okay . . . "

But the bear didn't seem convinced. He continued to sniff the air and study the unfa-

miliar children. Slowly, he began to rise on his hind legs. As he lifted his hulking frame to stand he seemed bigger than ever.

"Oh, God, help us," Ryan whispered.

"Marlene, stand right by me and raise your arms as high as you can reach!" snapped Ryan. He bit his lip and grabbed Billy and lifted him to his shoulders. "Raise your hands up, Billy, but don't make a sound."

Ryan desperately tried to sound reassuring as the three continued to slowly back away from the bear. "It's okay, bear. It's okay."

"My arms are getting tired," whispered Billy.

"Keep them up, Billy," ordered Ryan. "Slowly wave them from side to side. You, too, Marlene."

Ryan's neck and shoulders were throbbing from the weight of carrying his brother. He hoped and prayed he wouldn't trip as he carefully, slowly, backed away from the standing bear.

With a huge sigh of relief, Ryan watched as the bear dropped back down to all fours. They weren't out of danger yet, but apparently the nearsighted animal was losing interest in them because they seemed harmless. After one last sniff of the air, the bear turned and lumbered over to a rotten old log.

Cautiously, the children continued to back up to the trail. Since the bear was gone, they looked pretty silly walking backwards with their arms in the air and Billy still perched on his brother's shoulders. But they didn't care. They'd rather be silly and safe, than . . . . Ryan shuddered as he thought about how close they had come to real danger.

When they finally reached the trail, Ryan set Billy down. The little boy started running back to his parents before his feet even touched the ground.

"A bear! We saw a bear!" he shouted as he headed toward his parents. Greta ran to meet him halfway.

"Brave dog," said Marlene. It was the first words out of her mouth since the incident began. Ryan couldn't do anything but look at her, give a weak smile, and shrug. His heart hadn't slowed down yet. He was still trying to catch his breath, and tears kept coming to his eyes.

Mr. and Mrs. St. Pierre weren't sure whether Billy was making believe about the bear or not, although he certainly did seem convincing. It was when they saw the pale white faces of Marlene and then Ryan that they realized how real that bear had been.

There were some tears, plenty of excited laughter, and lots of hugs as the family went over and over the details of the encounter. Then they all sat in a circle and took turns praying out loud.

Mr. St. Pierre's prayer was long. He thanked God for his family, and for keeping them safe as they learned about the world around them. He asked God to continue to be with his children as they grew up. All the children looked at their father when he talked about meeting dangerous situations in the future. They certainly hoped there wouldn't be any more bear encounters any time soon.

Marlene thanked God for her big brother,

who acted calmly and sensibly throughout the encounter. She thanked God that Ryan was there when they saw the bear. She said, "And I think I've learned something about not being afraid. I mean, I'm sure Ryan was afraid, too, but he stayed calm. I'll think of that if I am in a dangerous situation again."

Mrs. St. Pierre thanked God for the wonderful world around them. "Today we've been reminded again that we don't own this mysterious and complex creation. It is Yours. You've only put us here to take care of it. Thank You for the responsibility, and help us to do a good job." She, too, thanked God for each member of the family and their presence of mind when danger was near. She hugged Billy tight on her lap as she prayed, and she cried tears of relief.

Ryan's prayer was short. "Thanks for being with us today, and thanks for my family."

Then it was Billy's turn to finish up the prayer and, of course, his was the longest. He thanked God for the mountains and the trees and for healthy bodies and nice weather and a good breakfast. When he could think of only one more thing to be thankful for, he began to finish up his prayer: "And thank You for Greta, who was fast enough to run away from the bear and not get hurt. She wouldn't have been smart enough to do what we did. And thank You for the food that the bear ate before we got there, so he wasn't hungry and grumpy. And thank You that we left all the food with Mom and Dad, so the bear couldn't smell any food on us when he was smelling the air. And thank You that we didn't trip as we were backing up, and that no hikers left empty pop cans for us to trip over. And thank You for the honey in the old log that smelled better to the bear than we did. Amen."

And everybody said together, "Amen."

As the family turned to head home, a forest ranger came by after an inspection of the watchtower. The family eagerly and proudly told the ranger about their bear encounter.

"Sounds like you did everything just right, kid," he said to Ryan. "Good for you! You talked quietly and made yourself as tall as possible to make the bear think you were bigger than he. Do you think you would have been able to out-growl him or stand your ground if the bear had decided to charge?"

Ryan smiled and looked at the ranger, "I guess I won't know that until next time."

Billy interrupted and announced he wanted to play the pretending game just one more time. So it was, that in the same grove where they did impersonations that very morning, Billy chose to act out his brother Ryan. He grabbed his teddy bear from his mother's backpack and flung it to his shoulders. With the floppy bear perched up high, Billy began to walk backwards and seriously whisper. "It's okay, bear. It's okay. We were just leaving. It's okay."

And it was.

OUTDOOR WORSHIP

You don't have to have a close encounter with a bear to have a worship service in the woods. You can worship God anytime, anywhere; but outdoors in His natural world can be an especially nice place. When Jesus needed some time to refresh Himself, He often headed for a quiet spot next to a lake, away from people. Find a quiet spot outdoors where you can be alone with Jesus or worship with your family.

Make plans for your time of worship. Include songs and Bible readings you enjoy. As you sit in your outdoor chapel, what do you see that reminds you of our Creator? What bit of nature reminds you of God's forgiving love?

Remember that when you are in a church building full of people, you are surrounded by God's creation as well. God created every one of those people around you, just as He created every plant and wild thing. God helps us care for *all* of His creation, people too.

A Place for Her Pony

Jess patted Jasmine's neck as she cantered the tall horse around the ring. "Just one more jump and we'll call it a day," she said. As she turned the chestnut mare toward the last jump, the perfect one-two-three rhythm of the canter was so smooth she almost laughed as she looked ahead over the fence. Jasmine picked the perfect spot, and Tess and her horse sailed over the fence as one.

Perfect! thought Tess' mother as she looked on from the kitchen window. She was thankful her 12-year-old daughter was now tall enough to ride her mare. She was even more pleased that Tess loved horses and horseback riding as

much as she did. Jasmine, short for All That Jazz, was going to be a perfect hunter jumper and a terrific friend for Tess throughout her teenage years.

It was almost dark when Tess came in for dinner. "How was your ride?" Mrs. Hamby asked.

"Okay," replied Tess.

"Just okay?" pressed her mother. "What's wrong?"

Tess had tears in her eyes. "Mom, Jasmine is just wonderful. I never knew a horse could ride so smooth. I guess I'm just used to Poco's shorter, pony stride, but . . . " she paused and swallowed hard. "Poco looked so sad when we passed her on the way back to the stable. She thinks I've deserted her." Tess rested her head on her folded arms at the kitchen table.

Mrs. Hamby knew well enough to just let Tess sort this out by herself, so the room was quiet for some time. The only sound that could be heard was the shower in the mud room. First it was on, and then it was off. On again, and then off for good. Tess knew it was her father, because nobody used less water than he did to get himself clean. She didn't even lift her head when he came into the kitchen.

"What's the matter with Tess?" he asked his wife.

When Mrs. Hamby explained, Tess' dad said, "Let's sell the pony. Let somebody else get some good out of her."

"Dad . . . " wailed Tess. She stood up and ran to her room.

She fell asleep that night without a solution for Poco's plight.

The next morning Jess was eager to tell Chris, her Sunday school teacher, about yesterday's ride. Chris was a horse person too. She had been competing in rated horse shows for some time.

Chris read from 1 Corinthians, "God is able to provide you with every blessing in abundance."

The words kept going around in Jess' mind. God certainly had blessed her. She had a wonderful family, a terrific house, and two horses!

As the rest of the class discussed ways to

increase their offering for their mission project, Tess started thinking about dear, sweet Poco. Chris interrupted her thoughts, "Yoo-hoo, Tess, are you with us today?"

Tess explained her problem. "Maybe Dad is right," Tess grumbled. "Maybe I just ought to sell Poco and give the money to our project. I wouldn't want to use the money for myself anyway." After a pause, she added, "But I don't suppose I'd be a very cheerful giver."

As usual, class was interrupted by adults streaming in to put on their choir robes. Chris took the weekly intrusion in stride, knowing that soon the building addition would be finished and she would no longer need to share her classroom with the choir.

As the kids left the room, Chris sent Tess a smile that seemed to say, "I know how you're feeling, and I wish I could help."

A little while later, when Tess was going over her flute music with the choir director, she saw her Sunday school teacher talking with her mother. They seemed awfully excited about something. Tess thought, Mom's probably bragging about my flute playing. I wish she wouldn't do that.

After the church service, Chris hurried to catch up with Tess. "I already asked your mom, and she said it was okay. How would you like to come with me to a special riding school I know about? I've got some friends I'd like you to meet, and there are some really terrific horses for you to see too."

Tess couldn't believe that Chris was inviting her to her stable! She knew that Chris had ridden in lots of rated shows. She even taught some riders too—riders that were much more advanced than Tess.

Tess would just have to not think about poor Poco for a while. She would think about All That Jazz instead, and her plans for her new horse. Maybe Chris could give her a few pointers about showing in rated shows. "I'd love to come," Tess finally answered.

The next Saturday, as soon as Tess got out of the car, she could see this wasn't a typical riding school. A class of four riders rode around the ring. Just outside the ring, a solid-looking ramp sat next to the fence. People walked alongside two of the ponies, ready to help the riders. (Tess would learn later that these people were called sidewalkers.) They were there just in case the riders lost their balance or needed help with their riding position.

"These kids have a disease called cerebral palsy," Chris explained. "They can't compete in sports like soccer or baseball, but they can learn to ride a horse. The disease affected their legs and hands, and in some cases, their speech. Sometimes cerebral palsy is only a physical disability; other times it can be a mental disability as well. These kids have been taking lessons for a long time. Now they are competing in horse shows."

It wasn't until the riders dismounted that Tess could see just how difficult it was for some of the kids to even move their legs and arms. While they were on horseback, she couldn't even see that they were disabled!

Tess watched the next group of four riders

get ready for their lesson. She could see that two of the riders had Down's syndrome. She had learned about that on TV. She and her mom had helped teach a special-education vacation Bible school class at their church. As the students in this class passed Chris, they gave her hugs and cheerfully said hello to Tess—even though they didn't know her. Tess couldn't help but smile back. Everybody seemed so friendly here.

These kids used the same ponies as the class before. Some leaders were walking in front of the riders directing the ponies with lead lines.

"These riders are still working on their position, voice commands, and leg work," Chris said. "When they learn all of those things, they'll be able to use the reins to direct their ponies themselves."

Tess took it all in as Chris went around and talked with the riders, volunteers, and parents. Chris taught classes here only on Saturdays and Monday nights, but she seemed to know everyone.

Back in the car for the long drive home, Tess told Chris how friendly everybody seemed. "It is not as snobby as some of the stables I've visited."

Chris smiled. "That's because everybody's working toward the same goal—to help these kids experience the independence and challenge of horseback riding. Everybody else has hobbies; why shouldn't these kids?"

Tess asked about all the ribbons and trophy photos she had seen on the bulletin board.

"These riders compete in Special Olympics and other shows for riders with disabilities," Chris explained. "And many of our riders compete in regular shows as well. The same skills that help these riders survive in the real world make them very tough competitors when they're on the horses."

An idea had been forming at the back of Tess' mind. "Could Poco be used at the riding school?" she asked. "They can borrow her to use in their classes."

Chris explained, "The program doesn't borrow horses. You would have to donate

Poco to the program for keeps." Tess would have to think about that for a while.

That evening, Tess and her parents prayed about the program. The enthusiasm, cheerfulness, hugs, and good care that the ponies received made the school seem like a perfect home for Poco.

It turned out that Poco was a wonderful horse for the school. She was patient and gentle. After a little special training, she was used regularly in classes, and even went to shows and demonstration rides. Tess began winning ribbons with Jasmine, but she became a regular volunteer at Poco's new home. She cleaned tack, groomed horses, and helped in the ring.

Tess remembered the abundant blessings Chris had talked about in Sunday school. Tess was giving to others, but getting lots more happiness in return. Tess smiled as she rubbed Poco's nose. "I guess when we share God's gifts, everybody gets blessed."

CELEBRATE YOUR GIFTS

Materials

- Unprinted sheets of newsprint
- Markers
- Scissors

You are a part of God's creation. Part of being a good steward of God's creation is using the gifts He has given you. Ask a friend or someone in your family to trace around your body as you lie on a large sheet of newsprint.

Write gifts that God has given you next to each related body part. You might write "caring" or "thoughtful" by your heart, "helpful" by your hand, "energetic" by your legs, "wonderful" by your smile, "good listener" by your ear. Ask friends or members of your family to write down gifts they see in you. Talk about how you can use your gifts to share the love God has given you.

Make body outlines for friends or family members and write down their gifts too. You may want to draw body shapes on small pieces of paper rather than using large newsprint.

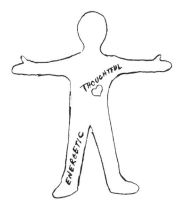

Albert Uses It All

The engine of the propeller plane purred quietly as three teachers flew across the bush country of northern Canada. Their pilot, Micah, had met them at the airport in Edmonton, Alberta. They had packed all their teaching supplies and two guitars between the seats of the small plane. From their cramped quarters they searched the trees below for any signs of life. Their destination now was a small village in the northwest corner of Alberta. Most of the people who lived there were either Inuit or Cree. A small population of white settlers also made their homes in the remote village.

In the winter the area was accessible by

frozen roads, but when the temperature was above freezing the roads were impassable. Only planes, landing on water, could provide transportation to and from the larger towns and cities far away.

Micah told the teachers about the general store he and his wife, Elizabeth, managed. Their store was also the post office and the bank. And Elizabeth was a nurse-midwife. They held Bible studies and worship services in their home.

Micah had arranged for the teachers to come to the village during the summer to teach a vacation Bible school. "Watch out for the fierce natives," he warned as they stepped off the plane.

With wide eyes, the teachers listened. Little did they know that the "fierce natives" Micah was describing were actually the huge, hungry mosquitoes who lived in this bush country.

The pilot had not been exaggerating. The attackers swarmed around the new arrivals as soon as they stepped on to the lake's shore.

It wasn't too long before the three teachers

noticed that people in this area were not con-cerned with time. The teachers woke up to radio alarm clocks and wore wristwatches. The people here did not.

On the first day of vacation Bible school, some children arrived over an hour early, oth-ers did not get there until just before lunch. The teachers put their wristwatches back in their suitcases.

Albert was always the first to arrive at Bible school and the last to leave. The teachers were able to share God's love with the curious boy as he helped them set up art projects and puppet shows. Soon Albert learned that Jesus loved him enough to die for him.

Albert invited his teachers to visit his home. There they met his grandparents, two uncles, and his mother. Albert's grandparents tended the garden, his mother took care of the house, and the uncles were hunters. They relied on the elk in the surrounding wilderness for meat, leather, moccasins, and even buttons.

Albert explained how the whole elk was used by the family. After a kill, the meat was

cured and stored away. The skin was tanned for leather using a long, natural process. The fat of the elk was rendered for lard, or tallow, for making soap. The fat also could be used as fuel for lamps.

The uncles used the leather to make moccasins and boots. They made enough for the family and plenty to trade and sell. The bones of the elk were dried and ground into bone meal for the chickens, and the internal organs were taken far from the house and fed to the cats. The chickens, in turn, provided eggs and meat, and the cats kept the mice away. Even the antlers of the elk were sliced thinly to make beautiful buttons. The uncles gave each of the teachers a pair of elk moccasins to take back to the States with them.

Too soon, it was time for Albert to say good-bye to his friends. He thanked his teachers for all he had learned about God's love. His teachers smiled. They had learned a lot, too, about a different way of life that respected God's creation.

SAND PAINTING

Using colored sand to add interest to a design can be a natural way to make a beautiful work of art that reminds us to respect all of God's creation and to use our resources wisely.

Materials

- Several colors of sand in separate containers
- White glue
- Art paper and poster board
- Pencil
- Large shallow pan to hold artwork while applying sand

Plan a simple picture that shows part of God's creation. Draw your design lightly with pencil on art paper. Choose the colors of sand you will use for each area.

Lay your design in the bottom of a shallow pan. Apply a thin layer of glue to all the areas you want to be a particular color. Then sprinkle that color of sand over the wet glue. Gently shake off any excess sand.

Set your picture aside and shake the extra sand from your shallow pan back into its individual container. Allow the glue to dry. Then put your design back in the pan and choose the next color of sand to use. Apply the thin layer of glue to all the areas that are that particular color, and then sprinkle the colored sand over the wet glue. Remember to shake the colored sand back into its individual container before moving on to the next color.

When your sandpainting is finished, add a Bible verse that reminds us to respect the earth that God created. You might choose: "God saw all that He had made, and it was very good" (Genesis 1:31).

Hazardous Matt

"That's a good idea, Paul. I'll have a talk with Matt right away. I'm sure sorry about all this. Yeah, okay. See you soon." Mr. Fay hung up the phone and walked to the back door.

"Matthew Fay!" he called loudly.

From the other side of the dirt pile, where he had been busily designing an entire highway system in miniature, Matt immediately poked up his head. He knew Dad was upset about something, because he had called him by his full name. As Matt hurried to the house, he tried to remember anything he had done during the day to upset his dad. He went through a checklist in his mind. Broken anything? Not today. Forgot to put Dad's tools away? Maybe. The bike in the driveway? Probably not. Report card? No, he got that bad news two weeks ago. A call from a teacher? Not expecting one today.

Matt didn't know why his father was upset, but he knew he'd find out right away. At the bottom of the porch steps, he looked up at his father to see if he could get a clue as to just how upset he was. Dad looked relaxed—no veins sticking out on his temples, no holding his head in his hands, not even a scowling look.

This shouldn't be so bad, thought Matt to himself.

"Come in here," his father said in an exasperated, but not angry, tone.

"I just got off the phone with Brian's dad."

"I can explain," started Matt, thinking that his dad had found out about the broken telephone.

"Brian is upset about what happened today," continued his father.

I'm going to get Brian for this, Matt told

himself. Why did Brian have to squeal to his father? It wasn't my fault that the phone broke. Well, maybe it was, but I didn't know it was a working phone when I started taking it apart. Brian should have stopped me. Couldn't he see that I was trying to get the magnet out of the mouthpiece? Brian knew we needed a magnet for our electromagnetic, anti-radioactive, toxicity-detecting sludge buster. Why did Brian bring that phone to me in the first place? Maybe Brian squealed because he was angry that I yelled at him.

Matt thought it would be best to just level with his dad, confess before being accused, apologize before his dad got all worked up yelling at him.

"Look, Dad, about their telephone. I'm sorry. I know I can get it back together."

His father interrupted him, "Their telephone? What happened to their telephone? I don't know anything about a telephone."

Matt winced. He knew he had blown it. He shouldn't have said anything. It was too late now.

"What happened, Matthew?" he demanded. Matt couldn't think of a believable story under pressure like this, so he told him the truth.

"Brian and I were trying to make an electromagnetic, anti-radioactive, toxicity-detecting sludge buster, but we needed a magnet." Before his dad could ask him to repeat all that, Matt continued, "I asked Brian if he had a phone, because . . . remember you and I took apart that old, broken phone and found a magnet inside? I thought maybe Brian had an old phone at his house. Well, he brought me one and I started taking it apart. The screws came out easily, but I had to pry the pieces apart with a screwdriver. Just when the frame cracked, Brian asked me what I was doing. He hadn't brought me an old phone. He'd unhooked the phone from their kitchen and brought that one to me! Honest, Dad. I didn't mean to break a working phone."

Before Matt had finished his story, his father had started rubbing his temple with his right hand. He's getting upset, thought Matt.

Mr. Fay shook his head, "Nobody told me about any phone, son. Brian's dad called here to say that Brian was upset because you called him a slimy glob of radioactive, mutated something or other."

"Oh, yeah," said Matt. "When I realized what happened, I called Brian a slimy glob of radioactive, toxic, mutated, hazardous waste."

Mr. Fay said he didn't need to hear the name again. "The point is, son, you and Brian broke something, and now you're mad at each other. All this needs to be worked out. Let's go over to his house together."

The discussion went better than either Matt or Brian could have imagined. Brian was in trouble because he had tried to hide the broken phone. But really, the fathers seemed more upset about the words the boys had used, than they were with the boys themselves.

The dads decided that the boys needed to learn what the terms they were throwing around meant. They planned a trip to a special kind of fire station.

On the following Saturday, the two boys and their fathers headed for Engine Company Number 4, the HAZMAT Unit in their area. This crew handled all fires, traffic accidents, and other emergencies involving hazardous materials. These men and women received special training in dealing with chemical fires, hazardous material, and first-aid treatment, and in precautions to take when cleaning up different chemicals.

Each rescue worker wore a special suit that looked just like a space suit, with a hooded face mask, huge gloves, and thick boots. These people had to be careful when dealing with dangerous chemicals. The boys were beginning to see that a little bit of what they saw in cartoons on TV was very real indeed. Their tour guide encouraged the two boys to ask questions, and they were full of them.

"If radioactive, toxic waste is dumped on a tiny animal, can it really change into a giant mutant, like on TV?" asked Brian.

The tour guide shook his head. "No, that won't happen. The animal would probably get very sick, though. It would depend on what exactly was dumped on the animal. There are all kinds of toxic chemicals in our world. There are some right in your own home." The boys looked at each other with wide eyes.

"Many of the accidents we have to deal with happen when trucks are delivering household products to a grocery store or garden center. Other accidents involve trucks carrying industrial-strength chemicals. Of course, we have to know what's in the truck to know how to handle the spill or explosion. Have you ever noticed the little signs that some trucks have in a sign rack on the back and sides of their cargo tanks? They tell us what type of chemicals are in the truck, so if there is an accident we know how to safely deal with it."

Matt and Brian wanted to learn more about the hazardous materials they had at their own homes. As they left the fire station, a rescue worker handed them a checklist for products to look for in their basements and garages, but reminded the two boys over and over to have an adult with them before they began to search.

When Mrs. Fay saw the checklist Matt and his dad brought home, she was shocked by the amount of dangerous products in their house. She knew the homes of their friends would be no different. In reading the papers that the HAZMAT rescue worker had given to Matt, Mrs. Fay learned that an even bigger problem was caused by the disposal of hazardous household products. When people had no need for a product any longer, they often would throw it away with the regular trash, or just dump it on the ground.

Mrs. Fay thought that hazardous waste from home would be a good project for Matt's scout troop. First she called Matt's scout leader. Then she called the phone number on the checklist and talked with a woman from an environmental services company. They talked a long time and made many plans.

Before long, Matt's scout troop was educating many people about the short- and long-term dangers of being careless with hazardous waste. They set up a booth at the fair and designed a pamphlet to give to people. They even helped set up a Household Hazardous Waste Collection Day to keep unwanted products from ending up in the county landfill.

When kids learned that words like "hazardous," "toxic," "radioactive" and such described very real chemicals with very real dangers, the cartoons they watched weren't so funny anymore.

The town's collection day was a wonderful success. The environmental services company took care of all the setup, collection, and removal of hazardous materials.

After the long day, the family drove home. Mr. Fay wondered out loud if the scouts had learned anything. Matt turned to his father as they got out of the car, "You know, Dad, I did learn something from all this."

"Oh yeah? What's that?" his father asked.

"Well, when this whole thing started and I told you the truth about what I had done, you didn't get nearly as upset as you do when I try to not tell you the truth. I mean, I tell you the truth about what I've done, and we work it out like two logical people. Pretty neat, huh?"

"Yes, that's neat, Matt. You know what would be even neater?"

"No. What, Dad?" Matt asked in all seriousness.

"If you two would stay out of trouble in the first place!"

Matt looked at his dad for a moment. "You know, Dad, I'll try that. But just remember, they don't call me Hazardous Matt for nothing!"

BE A HAZARDOUS WASTE DETECTOR

A hazardous waste is a discarded substance whose chemical or biological nature makes it potentially dangerous to people. A substance is toxic if it harms people when it enters the body. Highly radioactive wastes are unlikely to be found in a home, but radioactive wastes can be produced by industry and can cause illness if not handled properly.

The following materials contain hazardous waste. Make some phone calls in your community and find out how your family can dispose of them safely.

- **Asbestos:** A type of insulation that can lead to lung disease.
- **Toxic Metals:** Mercury, lead, arsenic, and cadmium.

- **Solvents:** Nail polish remover, paint thinner, dry-cleaning fluid, paints, polishes, some glues and adhesives.
- **Acids:** Car, camera, and watch batteries.
- **Bases:** Bases are the chemical opposites of acids. They, too, can be very corrosive. Lye (sodium hydroxide), oven cleaners, drain cleaners, and ammonia contain bases.

- Pesticides
- Used motor oil

- Brake fluid
- Engine degreaser
- Swimming pool acid
- Flea powder
- Chemistry sets
- Ammunition, powder, and primer
- Gun-cleaning solvent
- Antistatic brushes
- Photographic solutions
- Ceramic glazes
- Paint and thinners
- Aerosol cans of all types
- Spot remover
- Moth balls
- Expired medications
- Toilet bowl cleaner

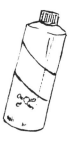

Simple Pleasures

Mrs. Natnick liked to hear her third graders at Good Shepherd Christian Academy discussing current events. The students enjoyed listening to each other and having someone listen to them. They took turns sharing their newspaper articles and asking questions.

Neil brought in a story about the energy crisis. The story was not very complete. It did not talk about hydroelectric power or nuclear power. Those are two ways we get electricity without burning a lot of oil or coal. The story did not talk about solar energy for cooking, electricity, and heat. It did not mention wind energy that is also used to make electricity. The newspaper article only discussed fossil fuels, and it said that soon there would be no oil or coal left. It did not say how soon "soon" was.

The students were worried about this energy crisis. Mrs. Natnick didn't want the children to worry. She wanted them to think. She told them to do two things for homework. The first was to find out what God tells us in the Bible about worrying. The second was to find out what God tells us about being greedy and wasteful.

The next day the class came to school and discussed what they had found out. "God doesn't want us to worry about tomorrow," Natalie shared. "He will take care of us."

"God doesn't want us to be greedy," Lucas offered. "He wants us to share with others and to take care of those who don't have as much as we do."

Mrs. Natnick told the class they did an excellent job with their homework assignments. But Kirsten wondered how it would help others if her family used less electricity. That was a tough question for Mrs. Natnick to answer. It

seemed very complicated.

"One simple way to help others," the teacher explained, "would be to figure out how much money your family saves by being careful with electricity and then donating that amount of money to a church or charity."

The class discussed ways to save electricity, and Mrs. Natnick wrote the ideas on the chalkboard. Everybody knew that turning off the lights when they weren't being used saved electricity. So did wearing a sweater in the house instead of turning up the electric heater. Brad even suggested keeping a big thermos of cold drinks on the counter, instead of opening up the refrigerator all the time.

Mrs. Natnick said there were lots more ways to use less electricity that could actually be fun for a family to do together. For example, sharing meals with another family saves energy because only one oven or stove gets heated up, and the lights stay off in one house after the family walks to their neighbor's house. Anytime you play a sport outside instead of watching television inside, you save electricity from the lights and the television. Mrs. Natnick said electricity could be saved by the family spending an evening together in one room reading books. Sometimes the parents could take turns reading, and sometimes the kids could read out loud. Some of the books could be old, family photo albums.

"My mom loves to bake," Carlos said, "but she does it all on one day during the week. She says she only has to heat up the oven one time."

"I'll have to try that," Mrs. Natnick said. "Here's a project to discuss with your family tonight. Think of three ways to use solar energy instead of electricity to save money on your family's energy bill."

The next day the students came to school full of ideas.

"We made sun tea," Kisha said. "We hung tea bags in a jar of water, and the sun heated the water instead of the stove."

Many students mentioned drying clothes on a clothesline instead of using an electric clothes dryer. Mrs. Natnick called a clothesline "a solar clothes dryer."

Trevor raised his hand. "After my sister washes her hair, she likes to dry it by sitting out on the deck."

Kent told the class about his father. "My dad's in the army. When he had to live in a tent in the desert, he used a black plastic bag filled with water to take hot showers. The sun heated up the water in the bag. Then he would hang the bag from a tall pole and let the hot water run out of a shower nozzle. When Dad got home, he built an outdoor shower next to the garage. He says it feels more refreshing than a regular shower." Some of the kids giggled.

Yvette said, "My family leaves the television off on Wednesday nights. We just moved, and we miss our old friends. Mom and Carrie and I sit down together and write letters and draw pictures to mail to our friends in our old neighborhood."

Before too long, the kids realized that using less electricity didn't have to be an unpleasant sacrifice. Mrs. Natnick explained,

"Thinking of creative ways to save energy can be fun. It can help you have a good time with your families. And, most important, it's a good way to care for the beautiful world God made for us. With simple pleasures, everybody wins!"

LAP-TOP DESK

Materials
- Clean, large pizza box
- Rubber cement or glue sticks
- Scissors
- Magazine pictures, family photos, and drawings

Pizzerias are usually willing to provide large, never-used pizza boxes for projects. Wrap the box in plain newsprint (often available at no charge from local newspaper printers), or decorate it with family photos, magazine pictures, or . drawings. Keep letter-writing supplies inside the box.

Include:
- Pens, pencils, and erasers
- An address book or several preaddressed envelopes
- Writing paper and envelopes
- Stamps
- Stickers or anything else suitable for decorating your letters

Not only will your lap-top desk store your letter writing supplies, but you can easily take it anywhere with you. Imagine how delighted your grandfather will be when your letter says, "Dear Grandpa, I'm writing this letter to you from the top of the hill where you and I hiked last summer to watch the sunset. . . . "

For a family project, make a lap-top desk for each family member. Plan a period of letter writing after a picnic in a favorite spot.

Heather's Haven

Heather was just tall enough to peek over the new deck and see her mom and dad studying the paint and wallpaper books. Mrs. Blair would smile and point to a pattern she liked, and Mr. Blair would frown and shake his head no. A few pages later, Mr. Blair would point to a pattern, but his wife would roll her eyes to the ceiling. Heather knew that meant "no way." She wished she could be in there helping them, but Mom had sent her outside.

Ever since Heather could remember, her mom and dad had talked about this house they were building. It would be the perfect house for their family. A big unfinished basement for a play room—big enough to roller-skate or ride a bike! There would be lots of bookshelves in every room, because all the Blairs loved to read. And it would be a house perfect for having lots of people over for dinners and parties. A wide deck would run along the whole south side of the house.

Although her family still lived in their small apartment, they had come out to their new house for the day to make final decisions about paint and wallpaper and such. Good thing the house is almost ready, Heather thought. The doctor had told Mom her due date was February 28. That would be only two weeks after their move to the new house! I'm more than ready for a brother or sister, Heather thought. I don't care which.

Heather turned away from the deck and looked at what was going to become a big backyard. She tried to imagine what the new yard would look like, but she was a little discouraged. In the garden apartments where they lived now, there was a wonderful little wooded park. In the morning and late afternoon you could see all kinds of beautiful birds. Big ones, little ones, all colors, and there were always squirrels and chipmunks around. The chipmunks were shy, but the squirrels had gotten quite tame. Since Heather hadn't had many other children around, she had spent a lot of time watching and getting to know the frisky nut-eaters. Their absolute favorite treat was puffed corn cereal. They would stand up and chatter like a wind-up toy when they saw Heather coming with the orange and yellow cereal box.

She was going to miss all those animals when her family moved. Although the Blairs had been careful to make sure the builder left the two big trees undisturbed, there wasn't much else in the backyard. Heather hadn't seen any animals in all the times they had visited the house while it was being built.

Later that evening, Heather rested her head against Mom's shoulder, thinking about the new home. She bolted upright, startling both her mom and dad. "But there are no animals!" she exclaimed. She looked at her surprised parents and explained. "For my whole life I've had squirrels, chipmunks, and 20 different kinds of birds in my backyard. Well…it wasn't my own private backyard; but right out my window were all these wonderful creatures. There aren't any at the new house. Our new backyard is lonely and boring."

Mr. Blair understood Heather's complaint. "A new yard is just like a new house," he explained. "You have to decorate it. Only instead of wallpaper and paint, you use natural things like plants and trees. I'll write down our landscaper's phone number. Call him in the morning and ask him what trees and bushes are best for attracting birds."

"I have a gardening book that may help," Mom said. "This is the best time to plan the yard, because spring is just around the corner. Let's make you the landscape researcher, Heather. Find out all you can about decorating the yard to make it inviting for many kinds of birds, and squirrels—and chipmunks too."

"There are deer in that area," Dad added, " and they ought to be invited to the Blair yard as well. You draw all the sketches and make all the plant lists, but leave space for my vegetable garden! I'll give you some ideas and help you with expenses and such."

Heather was thrilled. She took the garden book to her room and read as long as she could keep her eyes open. That night she dreamed she was in a beautiful garden surrounded by the wild animals she loved.

Night after night, Heather studied her garden book. She talked to the agricultural extension agent on the phone. She sent a letter requesting information from the National Wildlife Federation in Washington, D.C. She drew notebooks full of sketches and lists of plants, trees, and shrubs that would attract wildlife to their yard.

Heather and Dad planned to divide the yard into sections. The quiet side of the house near her bedroom window would be a special bird area. Between the two sycamore trees, among the rock outcroppings, would be the squirrel, chipmunk, and jaybird area. Looking straight out from the house, between the rocky area and vegetable garden area, Heather had drawn in a children's play area complete with swing set, slide, and playhouse. Between the garage and the house was a nice area of lawn that stretched under the sycamore tree closest to the house. It would be a nice picnic area in the summer and, with the right plantings, it would be a wonderful picnic area for colorful songbirds and hummingbirds too.

The backyard was soon referred to as "Heather's Haven," and she spent hours learning how to use plants for food and shelter for birds and wildlife. Along the quiet east side of the house Heather wanted to plant trees that would provide food for birds and nesting areas too. She wanted to be sure there were no good hiding spots for neighborhood cats in this area. Since there was a water spigot on this side of the house, she added a birdbath to her sketch. She looked forward to waking up with the sun shining through her curtain and the sound of birds singing in the trees outside her window.

Heather's plans to attract chipmunks and

gray squirrels included planting oak trees for their acorns and some pine trees for their cones. With sunflower seeds and dry corn, Heather would add extra delicious reasons for squirrels and chipmunks to visit.

One night as Heather and Dad poured over their plans, Mom asked their opinion on a name for the baby they were expecting. "With the special yard you two are planning, there's only one perfect name," said Mom. "Adam if it's a boy, and Eve if it's a girl!"

Dad laughed, and Heather pictured the baby sitting on a blanket with all kinds of God's creatures around. Bunnies on the blanket, squirrels perched on a nearby stump, butterflies and colorful birds flying about. And inching along the baby's forefinger, being studied carefully by little Adam (or Eve) would be a caterpillar.

So the days passed. Soon it was February, and the Blairs moved into their new house. Before long Dad was calling Heather from the hospital, "Congratulations, Heather. You have a baby brother! Ask Grandmother to bring you to the hospital. He's big, and he's beautiful, and he wants to meet his big sister! Your mom is fine too. She wants to talk with you."

When they got to the hospital, Heather gave Mom the present she had brought for her brother—a book that she had made herself. It was called "Baby's First Book of Birds." Inside were delightful drawings of cardinals, chickadees, robins, finches, and every songbird that Heather hoped to attract to their yard. Mother gave her a big hug. Finally, Heather realized that nobody had said what the baby's name was.

"Do we have a choice?" laughed Mother. "His name is Adam! Adam Ethan Blair."

ATTRACTING WILDLIFE
TO YOUR BACKYARD

Whether you live in the city or the country, on a ranch or in an apartment, you can encourage all types of colorful, active animals to take up residence within view of your backyard windows. Even your school property can be enhanced to invite butterflies and birds, delightful squirrels, frogs, and lizards!

In areas where building and development have destroyed natural wild areas, habitat restoration is a critical need for wildlife. For an informative booklet on Backyard Wildlife Habitat and an application to certify your property (or the school's) as an official Backyard Wildlife Habitat, send a postcard to:

Backyard Wildlife Habitat, Dept. BHI
National Wildlife Federation
1412 Sixteenth Street, NW
Washington, DC 20036-2266

You can also make a butterfly bucket for your backyard or balcony to invite colorful, fascinating butterflies to your home.

Materials

- Planting containers: Plastic dishpans, a window box, or several flower pots.
- Drainage tray: To prevent excess water from making messes or dripping on neighbors below your balcony, place an old cafeteria tray or a styrofoam meat tray under your planting container.
- Gravel: To provide necessary drainage within the planting container.
- Potting soil
- A small pie pan or shallow bowl to hold a fresh water supply for your invited butterflies
- Seeds and starter plants: A wide variety of flowering plants provide nectar for butterflies and even hummingbirds. Top choices are butterfly weed, cardinal flower, zinnias, marigolds, purple coneflower, lantana, and garden phlox. Lavender and the Mexican sunflower also attract butterflies and colorful moths. Check with a seed catalog or garden shop to see which flowers grow well in your area.

Line your planting containers with an inch or two of gravel. Add potting soil to fill within an inch of the top of your container. Place flowering plants in your container first. Allow enough room so that grown plants won't become overcrowded. Plant seeds according to package directions in space available. Leave a space for your water dish.

Place your butterfly bucket on your drainage tray. Water thoroughly and wait. Be sure to check daily for water.

Up the Downstream

Our first trip down the stream had gone perfectly. My dad had a tube; so did my brother, and so did I. The weather had been perfect—hot sun, cool water. Dad took us down the Little Antietam Creek for that first trip. I had just bobbed along, letting my fingers make ripples in the water, sitting back in the tube, gazing at the beauty of this wilderness area through the frame that my old sneakers made in front of me. I thought that tubing would be a terrific way to spend every sunny afternoon. What a great way to see places and animals we wouldn't ever be able to see on foot!

If we had known then just how disastrous

our second trip would be, we probably would have hung up our tubes for good. My brother and I still feel bad about scaring our parents like that and making everybody worry for hours and hours about us. Here's what happened.

On the second Saturday in June, we anxiously listened to the weather report for the next day. Father's Day was expected to be hot, clear, and beautiful! Perfect tubing weather. Everybody would be gathering at Grandpa's for the day. Willy and I had decided to take garbage bags on this trip and pick up litter as we walked our tubes back to the starting point. Most of our cousins were too young to go on our cleanup tube trip, but my cousin John had just turned nine, and he was on a swim team. He would be able to go with us.

It was so hot on Father's Day that we decided to eat fast and then load up the truck with our supplies so we could hurry down to the cool creek. You should have seen the truckload of people headed to the creek. There were aunts and uncles, all kinds of cousins and, of course, Grandpa. Grandma and John's mom had stayed at the house. So had my Uncle Bob.

Dad said that now that I was 13, I could be the guide. I would be in charge. He gave strict instructions to Willy and John that they had to listen to me.

We grabbed three tubes and our empty trash bags. John reached down and grabbed Allie. "She's a little dog. She can sit on my tube," he said. I didn't even notice he had her until it was too late to send her back. We took off with everyone on shore waving good-bye.

With our feet pointed toward the sky, we laughed and carried on as we floated on and on and on down the stream. We'll never know how long we were floating, but we had gone a lot farther than we did the last time.

"Let's head back," I finally said. "Get off your tubes and start walking."

That's when things started to go wrong. John had forgotten his shoes and said he couldn't carry Allie and push his tube and walk barefoot on the rocky bottom all at the

same time. So I pushed my way over to him and took Allie.

The stream was deeper, much deeper than where we had been when Dad was with us, and it took more effort to walk against it. Allie had liked the ride down, but she seemed nervous about this upstream business. I held her in my arms, but every once in a while she'd squirm and scratch my bare skin. When I tried to put her down, the current started to carry her away, and I had to grab her by the collar to save her.

John was having a terrible time with the rocks and kept falling behind. When he scratched his leg and stubbed his foot on a branch underwater, he told us he quit. He just couldn't go any farther.

So there I was, downstream farther than I wanted to be with a brother who kept wanting to hurry ahead of us, a cousin who was about to give up, and a dog in my arms that wouldn't hold still and kept scratching me. I wanted to cry, but I didn't.

"John, you get on this tube and hold Allie,"

I ordered. "I'll pull you two and push my tube. Willy, you slow down. We're probably already in trouble for being gone so long, and we'll be in more if you lose your balance in this deep water and we're not there to help you."

Willy muttered something about sisters and being able to take care of himself, but he did what I ordered. Maybe he was getting a little worried like I was.

My great idea didn't work out for very long. I just wasn't strong enough to pull John's tube with him and Allie on it, and Willy just kept getting farther and farther ahead of us.

"Wait! Willy, wait!" I called, but either he was ignoring me or the stream was too loud for him to hear us. He kept going.

"Dear God," I prayed, "watch over Willy, and give him energy to get back to Mom and Dad so they can help us. Please, God, don't let anything happen to my brother."

I told John that we had to stop for a while. Maybe I could pull him farther if I just rested for a few minutes. As we sat along the side of the creek, I noticed that neither John nor I had our trash bags any longer. Not only had we not picked up any trash, but we had added to the pollution problem with two or three more empty plastic bags. Great.

Just then I heard Uncle Bob's voice calling to us from upstream. He kept calling, and we tried to call back to him, but he couldn't hear us. But I did hear Willy answer Uncle Bob. "Thank You, God. My brother is okay, and now we have help. Thank You."

I knew we had made some bad decisions, but I didn't know that my uncle's mistakes were going to get us into worse trouble, yet.

Uncle Bob had told Willy to stay where he was until he found us. And, when he got to John and me, I could tell he was relieved. He told us we looked like a pretty sorry bunch of waterlogged pups.

We started back with Uncle Bob pulling John's tube and me pulling my own tube and holding Allie. It was hard work. The current was just too strong. In a couple of places the water was up to my chin! We didn't know that when we were floating down the river! But that's why the water was running stronger, sometimes slow and deep, sometimes shallow and fast. I still don't know where Uncle Bob got the strength, but he just kept walking and pulling, pulling and walking.

Before long it started raining. John asked Uncle Bob, "What happens if there's lightning? My teacher says we're not supposed to be under trees or in rivers if there's lightning. What are we going to do?"

Uncle Bob knew John was scared. "Don't worry," he said. "God won't let anything happen that we can't handle with His help."

Suddenly Uncle Bob tripped, lost his balance, and tipped John and Allie into the water. I froze, but Bob grabbed Allie's collar and held John above the water until he regained his balance. I knew God was helping us at that point.

Uncle Bob talked to us, too, about God's guardian angels, and how our guardian angels were working especially hard to help us. I knew they were watching over us, but I was ready to get home.

After trugding upstream for hours, it started getting dark, and I wondered why we hadn't gotten back to Grandpa's. Later we realized we had taken the wrong fork in the stream and were working our way even farther away. Good thing our parents and relatives had started searching on foot and in cars. They had even called the police.

Just as we caught up with Willy, we heard cars driving on a highway across a bridge somewhere ahead of us. We pushed on until we made it to the bridge.

Uncle Bob yelled as we scurried up the bank to the roadside. "You guys be careful up there. I'm not going to spend all this time getting you out of the creek just to have you get hit by a car!"

As soon as we got to the road we knew where we were. We were still over two miles from Grandpa's house! We called Grandpa from a phone booth at a gas station, and he came and got us. Uncle Bob flagged down our dads as they were driving to different bridges farther downstream and talking to neighbors.

We got hugged and kissed and yelled at, but I was just relieved we'd made it. Of course, the first thing Willy and John said was, "We weren't scared at all."

Boys!

PUT LITTER IN ITS PLACE

Materials
- Plastic bag with zip-lock top
- White paper, slightly smaller than the height and width of the bag
- Markers, crayons, or construction-paper scraps
- Transparent tape
- Glue

Draw a picture about putting litter in its place. When you are finished, slide it into your litter bag, right side out, and carefully tape down all four sides. This is the front of your bag. On the back side of your bag, make a small slit about an inch long. Reinforce the ends of the slit with two small pieces of Scotch tape. Hang your finished litter bag anywhere people are tempted to litter. Check the bag and empty it when it is full.

A long-lasting bag can be made by covering the back of your picture with a piece of contact paper and then positioning it within the bag.

Dreams and Schemes

Mrs. Snider jumped! Her empty tea cup rattled against the saucer, as she hurried to the back door. Although she trusted her two sons, she didn't trust the ocean. At 12 and 14, they were too old to want their mother tagging along on their shoreline adventures, but Mrs. Snider was never completely at ease until they were back in the house. And the way her younger son, Lenny, was yelling, Mrs. Snider feared the worst.

"Ma! Hey, Ma!" Lenny called out again. The two collided in the hall as the boy barrelled through the kitchen. The shiny gold treasure in Lenny's hand fell to the floor. Lenny picked it up, and after he was sure it wasn't damaged he looked at his mother and said, "Mom, slow down. You're going to hurt somebody."

By this time Mrs. Snider had pretty well summed up the situation. Through the kitchen window she could see her older son, Gabe, meandering back to the beach house, stopping here and there to study who knew what along the shoreline. No one was hurt. No one had been washed out to sea. Obviously, Lenny had scared his mother half-to-death over an old watch he had found on the beach.

Mrs. Snider took it in stride. A few deep breaths, and she could remind herself that the boys had always respected the power of the ocean. They knew the family rules, and they obeyed them. She was the one that was the worrier. Mrs. Snider leaned over to study the watch with Lenny.

"I bet it's a Rolex watch," he said. "I bet it's worth thousands of dollars!"

"Maybe," his mother went along. "We'll ask Dad what he thinks when he gets here."

The Sniders had spent their summers at

this same beach house in Maine for the past eight years. Mrs. Snider and the boys stayed for the whole vacation, but their dad was a college professor. He could only come up between summer sessions and on weekends.

Every year the family returned to their bit of coastline, yet never was the shore the same. The surf continued to rush in, but no two waves were alike. The sealife and birds were always there, but never boring. Professor Snider liked to say, "God is the master composer. The steady rhythm of the waves provides a background for the unpredictable symphony featuring sky, birds, cliffs, and sea life. The symphony is yet unfinished." That's what Professor Snider liked to say.

"So," Mrs. Snider encouraged, "where exactly did you find the watch?"

After Lenny explained that he had found the watch in a tidal pool while Gabe was studying starfish, he asked his mom if he could keep it. He didn't want to wear it himself, but he thought he might be able to sell it to Mr. Jed, the gruff old man who owned the store out on the highway.

The sign in front of Mr. Jed's store said, "Antiques, maybe." Mr. Jed sold anything—anything he could sell for a profit. The Sniders liked to go to Mr. Jed's store on rainy days. He had shelves and boxes full of old stuff. Gabe liked to look around, but Lenny looked forward to the actual purchasing, because nothing in Mr. Jed's store had a price tag on it. You had to dicker with the old man himself to decide how much to pay. Lenny loved the wheeling and dealing.

"You can't keep the watch without making an effort to find the owner," Mrs. Snider told Lenny. "Why don't you make a couple signs, and we'll put one up at the gas station? You can put the other one closer to the beach where you found the watch. If nobody claims the watch within, say, a month, then I guess you can keep it."

Lenny clenched his fist. "Yes!" By this time Gabe had joined them in the house. "Think you found a treasure, huh, Lenny?"

"You never know, Bro," came the reply as

Lenny bounded up the steps in search of paper and the art box.

Gabe turned to his mother. "We ought to give Lenny an empty pillowcase to carry on the beach. He could bring home all kinds of junk that washes up on the shore."

Mrs. Snider nodded in agreement. Every time they went for walks they found something. Sometimes it seemed people deliberately left trash behind, but she hoped it was an accident most times, like when a paper plate blows away from a picnic. However it got there, Gabe was right. Junk didn't belong on the beach. Out loud she said that she didn't think she wanted all that junk at her house either.

"I like the treasures that you bring home, Gabe," referring to his beautiful seashell collection. "I'm just not so sure I'd know what to expect from your brother."

Later Lenny came into the kitchen carrying the signs he had made. Both of them were neatly written, but only had writing on the top half of the paper. Lenny explained that he was going to leave the signs up. As he found other valuables, he would just add them to the list. Whatever went unclaimed by the end of the summer he would sell to Mr. Jed. After a moment, he added to his idea. "You know," he said, "As long as I'm picking up stuff, I might as well pick up soft drink cans and glass bottles as well. A recycler will buy that from me, for sure!"

Mrs. Snider left the room and returned with two old pillowcases, one for each boy. "I wish they had drawstrings, boys, but I don't have any cord that would work for that."

The two boys looked at each other. They had learned how to make rope when they went to visit the seaport town of Mystic in Connecticut. They went outside with some yarn and were working on the rope project when their father drove up. With his help, they made a cord the way ropemakers used to make strong ship ropes long ago. Then they threaded the rope through the casing of the pillowcases, and their sacks were ready. They would set out first thing in the morning.

As they got ready for bed, Gabe looked forward to exploring the rugged outlands and shell-filled tidal pools during low tide. Lenny dreamed about the valuable treasures that he might find.

Downstairs their parents enjoyed a quiet evening together. Professor Snider was eager for tomorrow's hike. He had always been fascinated with the beauty and mystery of the New England shore. Exploring these wonders with his "dreamer" and "schemer" upstairs was the best way he knew to spend a summer Saturday.

Saturday morning Mrs. Snider watched her three adventurers fade away in the morning mist. Who knew what treasures they would find as they scoured the beach and celebrated the wonder of God's creation?

DRAWSTRING BAG

Materials
- Pillowcase
- Ball of yarn
- Scissors
- Cardboard tube (about 6–12 inches long)
- Pencil

Ask two friends to stand about 15 feet apart in an open space. Have one friend hold tight to one end of the yarn. Carry the ball of yarn to your other friend, carefully unwinding the yarn as you go. As the second friend holds tight to the yarn, walk the yarn back to the first friend.

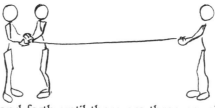

Walk back and forth until there are three equal strands held between the two friends. Cut the yarn. Tie one end of the three strands in a knot. Slide the knotted end through the cardboard tube. Slide the pencil between the strands of rope halfway between the knot and tube, as illustrated.

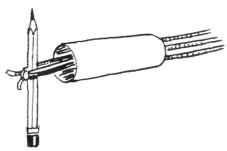

Turn the pencil around and around like an airplane propeller. Keep rotating the pencil until the strands are twisted tightly together.

With the twisted, unkinked line held straight and tight by your two friends, walk to the center of the cord and grasp it tightly. Have your two friends walk towards each other in a full circle, as illustrated, so that the line remains tight from where they are holding it to where you are holding it.

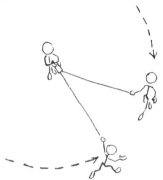

Have one friend give his/her end to the other friend. When he/she is holding both ends securely in one hand, and you are tightly holding the folded end, have your friend let go.

The rope should twist and coil to form your rope. (If it doesn't, it wasn't twisted enough with the pencil and tube.) Smooth out any kinks and tie a knot in the ends. This is your drawstring cord.

Carefully cut a small hole in the casing end of your pillowcase. Thread the cord around the pillow opening until the end comes out the hole. Tie both ends of the cord together. Close your bag by tightening the drawstring. Open it to collect treasures and recyclable items, or to put groceries in the next time you go to the market!

113

Tory's Bicycle Shop

"His mother goes on and on, but I'm sure James will be all right," Tory's mother said to his father. "Of course his bicycle is history," Mrs. Shane continued. "Mrs. Ehrhardt wants you to come up to the big house and get rid of that dreadful thing as soon as possible."

Mr. Shane said he'd get rid of the bike right after he got back from the meeting at church. He sounded tired. Mr. Shane was the handyman for the Ehrhardt Estate. He and his family lived in the gate house on the front of the property. The Ehrhardts lived in the huge stone house back farther down the lane. Both families went to the same church. Mr. Ehrhardt was president of the congregation, and Tory's dad served on the property committee. Both men would be at the meeting tonight, because they would be discussing the termite damage that had been discovered under the floor in the 100-year-old church. Something had to be done fast.

"What happened to James?" asked Tory as he grabbed a handful of cookies from the plate on the table.

Mother told him all she knew about James' bicycle accident. Apparently he had been going too fast when he turned off the main road onto the Ehrhardt's lane. The rear wheel had spun out from under him, and he skidded on his side into the driveway. The bike slammed against one of the huge oak trees that lined both sides of the driveway.

Tory knew how tricky that turn could be. He took it every day when he rode his bike to and from school. A hard rain would wash some of the gravel and sand from the driveway out onto the road. It was exciting to balance his bike just so and use just the right amount of rear brake to skid his bike around the turn, but it could be dangerous. Tory would often stop his bike after the turn to look back and see how long his skid marks were.

Tory shuddered as he thought about Mrs. Ehrhardt wanting to throw away James' bike. It wasn't more than a year old! It couldn't have been wrecked up too badly. Certainly it would at least still have some good parts on it. He asked his dad if he could bring the bike to his workshop instead of hauling it to the landfill.

Dad managed to smile. "Of course the bike will go to your shop, but don't you think you ought to see how James is doing? And be sure to tell him that you've got his bike. I'm sure it will be okay. His parents will just buy him a new one when they're ready anyway."

Tory nodded. He knew his dad enjoyed working for the Ehrhardts, but he did get frustrated with their attitude of always wanting brand new things.

Dad left for church, and Tory asked if he could go out to his shop for a while. His mom said okay.

Tory was the only kid in his fifth-grade class that had his own workshop for all his bike stuff. It was a small shed next to the garage. Inside was a workbench covered with tools and assorted bicycle parts, a special vise just for holding bikes, and, hanging on the wall, were wheels, handlebars, pairs of pedals, and all kinds of gears and chains for all sizes of bikes.

Tory would have loved to have a brand-new bike, but he knew that was pretty far down on his parents' list of priorities. Tory was saving his own money to buy one, and he went to bed most nights reading through bicycle catalogs and magazines. He knew just the one he was saving for, but in the meantime he rode the fastest, strongest bike around, even though it looked kind of funny. He and his dad had assembled it from bikes that Mr. Shane brought home from yard sales and flea markets.

When Tory was out riding by himself, he was proud of the machine he and his dad built. Mr. Shane called his bike "a custom design." But every time Tory pulled up in the schoolyard, he hurried to get his bike locked up under the stairwell where no one would see it. Anyone could see that the blue handle bars were from a mountain bike, the red frame was an old, heavy, stingray type, and the tires were the same size, but mismatched. The seat was held together with duct tape, and there was no kick stand. Tonight, Tory's plan was to replace the seat with a newer one.

Dad got home from the meeting at church and reported that the termite damage was pretty bad. The estimated cost to repair the floor of the little stone church was nearly 25 thousand dollars. A lot of money for their tiny congregation. There would be a special meeting after church on Sunday to discuss the crisis with the whole congregation. The church service would be held in the Sunday school room because the floor was torn up in the sanctuary.

Before Tory left for school the next morning, Mom gave him a basket of cookies and fruit to take to James. He left his bike leaning against the shed and headed up to the big house. He walked past the front entrance and around to the back door. Mrs. Ehrhardt greeted Tory and thanked him for the basket. She invited Tory in to see James, who was resting in the atrium.

He walked into the sunny, plant-filled room and found James lying on a wrought-iron chaise lounge. He was surrounded by pillows and had a pitcher of water on the table next to him.

Tory waved and asked, "How ya' doing, Speed Demon?"

James shook his head and muttered something about not really being hurt at all. Tory didn't know if James was more embarrassed by the wipe-out, or by all his mother's pampering.

"Hey, that turn is a pretty wicked one," started Tory, but James quickly interrupted.

"I've watched you take that turn hundreds of times," declared James. "I was just trying to make my back tire spin like you do. How do you make those long skid marks?"

Tory was surprised by the tone of admiration in James' voice. He never realized anybody was watching him. He was just having fun. He told James that he'd be glad to teach him, just as soon as he was better.

"My mom will never let me get another bike," James stated flatly. "She already threw the old one out. She can't stand to have anything that's scratched or damaged. I guess I'm lucky I was wearing a helmet and pads. If I had been hurt badly, she probably would have just thrown me out and gotten a new son!" He was able to laugh a bit at that idea, but he really started to sit up when Tory told him that his wrecked bike was in Tory's shop.

Tory suggested they fix the bike up together, and then Tory could teach James how to be a better rider. Suddenly Tory realized he had to leave right away or else he would be late for school. He jumped off the back steps and ran back to his house. He hopped on his bike and pulled it away from the shed in one motion and then flew down the driveway to head toward school.

As fast as he was able to go, Tory could see that he was going to be late. All the bike spots hidden under the stairwell were taken, and only one spot was left in the bike rack near his classroom. He locked up his bike and ran for the door. The tardy bell rang just as Tory slid into his seat. He rolled his eyes and moaned as he looked out the window and noticed how his odds-and-ends bike stood out from the rest, especially with the new florescent green seat he had put on the night before. He prayed that no one else would notice it.

It wasn't until a man with a big lion puppet showed up at the door that Tory remembered that there would be a guest speaker in class today. Tory was relieved any time there was something special that interrupted the regular school day. Every subject was his worst subject.

Today's speaker was from the county's recycling office. He used the puppet to help him teach the students about "Reduce, Re-Use, and Recycle." Every time the lion said "Reduce," "Reuse," or "Recycle," he would make a long growling sound for each letter *r*. The lion reminded the students of ways to

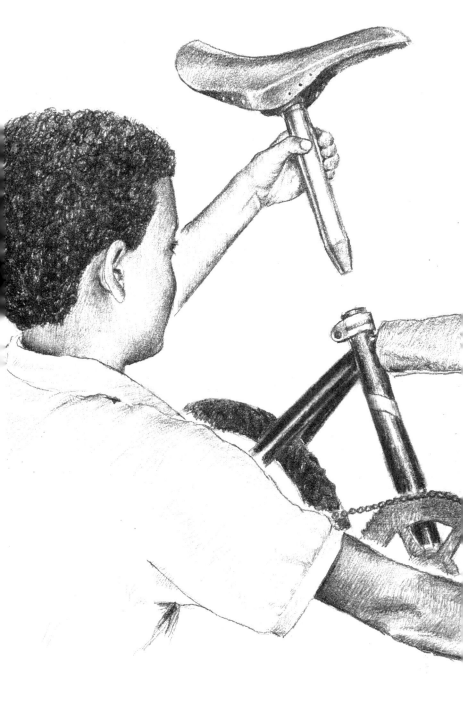

reduce the amount of trash they threw out by using fewer throw-away products, like paper towels and cups. Everybody already knew about recycling newspaper, aluminum cans, and glass, so the puppet moved on to talk about how we can reuse products to take better care of our natural resources and make less trash.

Nobody could think of an example, so the man asked the lion. The lion looked out the window. Tory realized the lion was looking right at his bike. He wanted to crawl inside his desk, but the lion said, "Say, there's a r-r-r-really ter-r-r-iffic example of r-r-r-reusing usable bike parts to make a r-r-r-eally r-r-r-radical new bike. Look at the bike on the end with the gr-r-r-reen seat! There must be parts of four or five bikes used to make one cool, custom r-r-r-acer. I bet that's the fastest bike around!"

"It is!" called out two or three other bike riders in the class.

Tory spun his head around to see who admired the speed of his bike. Didn't they realize that he always left school in a hurry because he was embarrassed by the looks of his homemade bike?

The lion went on to say that it was ingenuity like Tory's that was going to safeguard the future of our planet earth. He made it sound like Tory was going to save the world or something. At recess a group of admirers gathered around Tory's bike. They were full of questions that Tory answered gladly.

Tory rode home that afternoon feeling so proud that his wheels didn't even touch the ground. In the morning James had admired his riding ability. In the afternoon his class had noticed his bike. Never before had Tory felt as if he had any ability worth admiring. He felt great. He looked forward to working with James to help him get his bike on the road.

Then he thought about Mrs. Ehrhardt. He had told her that James' bike was in his shed, like his father suggested, but was she going to allow James to work on it?

He found out soon enough. James was waiting for him next to his bicycle shop. He said his mom didn't think they'd ever get the bike in a workable condition, so of course he could tinker with it. Mrs. Ehrhardt was underestimating the skill and determination of the two boys.

After a month of hard work and endless searching through boxes of derailleurs, brake cables, and gears, the 10-speed bike was ready for a road test. The boys had even bought some bicycle paint. Mr. Shane had helped them to prep and paint both their bikes. They both looked brand new. Before the boys were able to try out their workmanship, James brought out a gift-wrapped box that he had hidden for Tory.

Tory looked surprised, but hurried to unwrap the gift. Inside was a safety helmet, knee pads, elbow pads, and a racing jacket. Now Tory could dress the part of the bicycle genius that he was. He hurried to put on his new equipment, and the two jumped on their bikes and pedaled away.

The next Sunday, Tory and James sat in church together. James' dad stood up after the sermon to introduce the rededication of the sanctuary. He began speaking about the determined way Mr. Shane had worked to get the termite damage repaired, "Never once did Mr. Shane wring his hands and say, 'How can we fix this?' or 'It's hopeless.' No, Mr. Shane learned of the damage and said, 'This is what we need to fix this, and let's get to it.' The original estimate was almost 25 thousand dollars, but Mr. Shane organized people and materials and worked with the contractor to get the job done for a third of that. And not only did I see the floor get fixed, but I watched relationships develop and strengthen. This house of God is more than just a building. It's a history of the people's ministry within this building.

"I used to feel that Mr. Shane was my employee," Mr. Ehrhardt continued, "but now I feel that we are co-workers in God's service. I feel proud to know a man who practices a 'Just-Do-It' kind of attitude. He and all of those who helped are certainly doers of the Word and not hearers only."

Tory smiled at his dad and then at James. It looked like two generations of Ehrhardts and Shanes were friends and partners. Mr. Ehrhardt asked the congregation to join him in prayer. Tory bowed his head and breathed a quiet thank-You prayer of his own.

BIODEGRADABLE WRAPPING PAPER

Materials
- Unprinted newsprint
- Non-toxic poster paints
- Sponges cut in a variety of shapes
- Pans to hold paint
- Rags for cleaning up spills
- Newspaper to protect work area

Rolls of unprinted newsprint are often available free of charge from your local newspaper printer. Call your newspaper and ask about the ends of rolls.

Cover your work area with newspaper. Unroll the newsprint. Pour a bit of paint into the bottom of the paint tray. Dip the sponge in the paint. Do a practice print on scrap newspaper and then apply to the newsprint. Re-ink sponge as necessary. Allow paint to dry thoroughly before rolling up your new wrapping paper.